V. Nghiem

The Dance of Time & Power

story.one – Life is a story

1st edition 2023
© V. Nghiem

Production, design and conception:
story.one publishing - www.story.one
A brand of Storylution GmbH

All rights reserved, in particular that of public performance, transmission by radio and television and translation, including individual parts. No part of this work may be reproduced in any form (by photography, microfilm or other processes) or processed, duplicated or distributed using electronic systems without the written permission of the copyright holder. Despite careful editing, all information in this work is provided without guarantee. Any liability on the part of the authors or editors and the publisher is excluded.

Font set from Minion Pro, Lato and Merriweather.

© Cover photo: Photo by Taylor Leopold on Unsplash

ISBN: 978-3-7108-6766-8

To Farah and Gigi

You're my Time. You're my Power.

CONTENT

The Dance of Time and Power	9
The Celestial Animals	13
The Creator	17
The Intruder	21
In the Garden	25
Foxglove & Wonder	29
Dream	33
Terror	37
Nightmare	41
A Girl On A Boat	45
The Squire of the Forest	49
Dream's Price	53
The Day of Skyfall	57
Epilogue	61

Story 1
THE DANCE OF TIME AND POWER

The Dance of Time and Power

This is how the story always goes. Time fell in love with Power.

At the beginning, there was nothing. The nothingness contained only the cosmic entities, those of the primordial beings; Time, Power, Love, and Hatred. They roamed freely and alone through Darkness. Darkness was just that. Vast, old, and weary.

Until, long ago, Time and Power met. Upon their encounter, they danced. A dance of creation that brought Life as an explosion of elements. Fire, water, air, earth, and the varieties of sub elements formed from this dance into everything. Land masses were formed, then rivers and oceans wrapped them into the shape of nations. Everything was a creature of Life, until there was a group of organisms that learned to walk. They soon roamed the face of the earth, exploring and understanding the rules of nature. They started giving names to each other as a desire to find the commonalities and the differences. Animals were separated from humans. And humans evolved into elves, ogres, dwarves… With evolution came consciousness. Consciousness divided the creations of Power from the primordial forces.

Consciousness was to know the dance of Time and Power had to stop at one point. Time was once a constant, harmonic flow. Yet ever since it fell in love with Power, it became unpredictable. Time stopped flowing in one dimension and started rebelling with everyone's individual perception. Power loved this. Power was chaos at its purest form. It yearned to possess all beings.

This concerns everyone in the animal kingdom. The Council of Life had meetings long into the night and concluded that one of them had to go. They ambushed Power and ripped it apart. From Power's body, five elements were born: Fire, Water, Air, Earth, and Spirit. To ensure that Power would not reform, the Council of Life each took one element with them. The elements lived within the Council members, creating the four Celestial Animals: Fire Qilin, Water Kraken, Air Dragon, and Earth Mammoth. However, none of them was fast or strong enough to possess Spirit. So, Spirit lived freely without any forms.

Spirit, being a free element, settled to be the King of all Gods. The creatures of Braia believed that Spirit gives the powers and matches them to Wielders, creating the first generation of humans that could wield Elemental Powers.

The Celestial Animals

With a fraction of Power within them, the Celestial Animals became the symbols of Power at its purest, but most fractured forms. They understood that to master the pure form was to allow chaos to return to the realm. Each of these animals took with them the element and spread out to the world, handing the gifts to others. For a long time, they all lived like that, until a human discovered something inside her. She realized that the element, that was gifted to her, did not merely create her; it could also work for her. She shared this information with fellow humans and together, they unlocked the Wielding ability.

The Celestial Animals recognized the inert danger to this ability. To stop the spread of learning, they gave the humans another element in their sleep. When they woke, the pure elements had been broken and dulled into another form. Humans carried on to have the Wielding ability, but their Power had been changed forever. The knowledge did not just stay with the humans, but the wielding ways of other races are not the same. Their elemental powers are more closely linked to the nature and environment that they were born in. Trolls have rock-like skin, mermaids' skin helped them breathe underwater. Meanwhile, humans could transform and use the elemental powers to create.

Time danced on. In the infantry of the Braia continent, the races and species exist in tribes and communities. They did not have a country, just a rough border of territories between different political powers. The political powers are often leaders of the community, they have the right of land and of their own people. The world has carried on like this for a long time, where humans, elves, nymphs, trolls lived together. They all had the right of the land to their home.

However, fights and disputes between communities were inevitable. It was during this time that some humans stood up to unite the communities of one area into a nation, so they would have a better defense toward a bigger threat. These humans became the first authority figures, for instance, the Kahasadian Emperor or the King of Aler. During this time, the noble Houses started to be formed. Historians of the six Houses, that later on known as the Hexagon, researched a way to extract and wield pure elemental power. They succeeded and became the most influential Houses in each nation.

As Time danced on, histories became myth. But every creature of Life is a creature of Braia, and it will remain so until the Day of Skyfall.

Story 2
FOXGLOVE & WONDER

The Creator

I bring the rain like the clouds plague the sky.

I speak to birds and guide their wings to fly.

I hum the tune that you hear on the breeze.

I call the names of the stones and the trees.

In return, I am confined in this prison made of stones. Block by block, they imprisoned me into this man-made wilderness that rose like an ugly blotch of ink splashed against the blank space of an unfinished parchment.

They want me to stop creating because they fear the knowing.

They want me to stop drawing because I don't just draw them flowers. I drew the creatures of the dark and the worms that fertilize this soil. They fear whatever doesn't look like them.

They fear me.

Where I am, I do not know. I am just a gardener in the crop of life, one that was restricted to only a square of land, a chain on the power courses through me.

In my castle, solitude befriends me.

It brings me no gossip, no laughter, no glimpse of humanity, but it is mine. It brings me a false confidence to strive in this hall that leaves no echo, no voice, no visitor.

Not even ghosts would come to me.

In this impenetrable fort, the only thing that yearns to break is the silence. I haven't spoken for so long, I forgot how my voice sounds.

I wish I remembered the day you came. But the truth, my dear, is that a person standing at the beginning of the rest of their life has no idea that it has already started.

Sometimes their life reduces to the bony frames of a mortal body, standing erected and intrusive in their garden of flowers. You told me you sneak in through the back door, but I knew such things do not exist because they do not allow me to pass through. You just appear there like a manifestation of nature, unexplainable, unbound.

You stood in the garden of my life like you always belong there.

And perhaps you do.

You did the moment you came.

The Intruder

The tall grass around you whistled in the wind, rejoicing "You're here! Welcome home! The rightful owner!" The flowers turned toward you with their arms raised up, they chanted, begging you to pick them.

You look like *them*.

You were made of flesh and bones. I am scared of the arrival of you. The implication of your presence.

And you were lovely, so I am wary of you.

The mask hangs awkwardly on my face like it is too big and too small at the same time. Lately, I have learned that not everything is mutually exclusive. Big and small. Fear and courage. Love and hate.

I met you in my mask, and you didn't even step back.

Who are you?

"I could ask you the same."

I am the creature of the earth, said I, because perhaps that was all I am.

If I am being honest, my dear, my brush could create a whole universe. But I can only touch the tangible realm. For a moment, I wondered if I created you in the mist of my loneliness. Only after I talked to you did I know I couldn't have. I cannot create fearlessness and empathy and the unapologetic innocence that burst through you and claim you to be you.

I am not that powerful.

Heed my warning and leave, I said, and you ignore.

"You have beautiful flowers here. I need them. I will bring you flowers from other places in return."

But the only thing you bring me is the aching pain of a kindred spirit. A reminder of heat on the skin of those that had been out in the cold for too long. Some things are good for you and still hurt you. Things can exist at the same time, have I not said so?

I ask who you are because I need to know your identity.

You ask me who I am because you want to understand my soul.

In the Garden

I am just wearing the old bones of those who had fallen on this soil.

"Aren't we all?"

Uncertainty written across my eyes and you continue.

"We are every soul that lives through us."

Forgive me, for I cannot wrap my ancient brain around it. Not that I don't know what you mean, but I cannot understand the positivity in your voice when you spoke about leaving. As if everything you do is just a part in the grand scheme of things. And I want to be the grand scheme of things.

You want blue flowers, so I paint you blue flowers.

You want petals that look like the trumpet, so I make them too.

The only thing I ask in return is for you to not smile at me.

In the garden, I wear my mask and you wear your flowers. We stood together listening to the screaming of the wind. The wuthering heights threatened to snap and blow us all away. Yet you smile and in your eyes I find the calmness for my driftwood life.

You reached for me and in your hands held the secret to the rise and fall of civilization, the love and jealousy that tore mortal souls apart. You moved the stars into the ocean and watched it rise under the string of the harp.

Wonder is what you are to me.

But I, too, fear the unknown. Maybe I am no difference than the men that imprisoned me here.

In the end, I could not let my mask fall. Because my face, like the rough and swollen blisters on my hand, could only bring terror to those who cast eyes on it. I am the ugly blotch of ink splashed against the flowers you laid bare.

But I still want you.

To want is often more dangerous than to need.

One needs self-less things. One wants selfish things.

To want you is to be vulnerable enough to admit that you have perpetually changed my life the moment you stepped in it.

Foxglove & Wonder

I can make and change every tangible thing, but not myself.

I can't show you me. I can't give you me. Even if I know your hand might perhaps be the closest thread I have to reality.

Wonder is a sly one. To be wonderful, you continue to be unpredictable.

Because I befriended solitude, I do not receive words in the wind like most people. But the flowers call for me. It tells me to get out of my shell and run to town, a place I have never known, let alone touch.

If they hate me one, they hate wonder ten.

You never tell me the true nature of your activity, why you collect these flowers. In truth, I never knew if the flowers could do anything until you gave them that ability. But your giant heart is misplaced when you use flower's magic to heal.

I created so they imprisoned me.

You heal so they execute you.

When I arrived, it was too late. Wonder is a mortal flesh that slacks on a plank. Wonder is red blood dripping the stones. Wonder is mortal under the blade of men.

Even in the end, I couldn't let go of my mask. Perhaps the mask, too, has become too much of a part of me. A part of me that grew with you, touched by you, loved by you.

Stay with me.

"I can't."

Your refusals are a blunt knife that keeps poking at me.

Does it hurt?

How about now?

Stay with me, I repeat.

"If I ever find a way, I am only delaying the inevitables."

So you left.

How do you write about a person leaving? Do you include how your traitorous heart shatters into millions of pieces? Do you imagine taking flight or do you simply see their image shimmering in the sunlight?

In truth, a person never truly leaves. Your body may lay down, and you may become one with the earth. But I'd be the certainty of the sun rising to the unpredictable cycle of the moon. I'd be the water that blunt the rock. I'd be the last red thread in the lost myth of true love.

I will lay in the muddy road as time passes me by.

When you return, the road will be filled with foxgloves.

Story 3
DREAMSCAPE

Dream

Dream is a servant of Terror. Most people do not understand it, but the reasons are simple. While the Celestial Animals touch the tangible realm and Love touch the human emotions, Dream titters between the tangible and intangible, the real and unreal. Dream invades people's subconscious and guides them to the realm of the unknown, to take a dip in their daydreams, and ride the waves of their nightmares. Dream is Time. Because only in the dreamscape can Time tie itself into a circle. The past blurs into the presence into the future. An insect was old before it was born. A castle runs for miles but to travel only takes a few steps. A dance floor was pitch black with illuminating candlelights.

Dream is a servant of Terror.

Terror protects the dreamscape from being penetrated by the deities that fail to understand it. Terror is a guard and a queen to her suppliant's realm, because she is born inside that world. Part of Terror was created in the midst of the war of Love and Hate, part was born in the slaughter of the Celestial Animals, but the heart of Terror has always belonged in dreamscape with Dream. She commands the creatures to thrive and to break the barriers that are created by those inferior to them. Terror is a part of life. To be more exact, Terror is a part of *growth*. Without fear, humans would have never learnt that language of fire. Without fear, birds would have never touched the sky.

Dreamscape is a honey river flowing toward the waterfall. Dreamscape is a mountain range made up of a thousand butterflies. The butterflies are skeletons of forest creatures, dusty wings that sprinkle in the eyes of travellers with hallucigen powder. In the hall of Terror, obsidian pillars rise into trees and branches weigh down with the sunlight that is trapped between the cage of their fingers. A river runs in between them, reflecting the lilac light that glows into a golden orb in the middle. At the end of the river is a staircase that leads to the throne of Terror. The throne sits so high up that they can see the cloud from here. They are lush green with red embers burning at the core. The moons are the size of an arching door, inviting the creatures of dreamscape to pass through.

Welcome to dreamscape, where physicality was just a mere manifestation of imagination. And those who dared to dream were most rewarded.

Terror

"I think we can last forever."

Dream knelt in front of the throne. If Dream is the rightful creator of dreamscape then Terror is the queen of Dream. Terror and Dream are tucked away in the safehaven of their world, where they could be entirely their monstrous and terrifying selves. Terror arched her feline curve as Dream kisses her down the column of her neck. Colours burn behind the eyelids like a forest fire.

"I'm afraid everything will disappear."

"Just trust me."

In Dream's arms, sometimes they are the howling of the wind, sometimes they are bloody men in battles that just lost the last thread of humanity, sometimes they are the waves of the stormy ocean and the yawning grave in darkness.

Most of the time, they are women. Nothing could ever be as terrifyingly powerful as women.

"I am your lamb."

Dream wrapped her teeth around the inner thigh and dragged her mouth along the sweet and velvet flesh. I am your lamb, she said, and I am your wolf. She would swallow up Terror and drink in the woodland spirits that escape her throat. She would collect the prize and then she would serve.

No one ever understood the full extent of dreamscape's power. Dreamscape is not created merely from the ribcage of Dream. Dreamscape is a collective realm constructed by unwilling creatures of Life. Dream uses them as transportation to travel from one place to another. She finds the fabric that stitches realities together and pulls at the threads until the whole thing crumbles down. Then she would simply slip into another world, sometimes quiet like a monarch, sometimes as loud as a marching band.

With Terror, Dream takes her everywhere she demands. They roll in the dark haze cloud until it dissipates and the two bodies free fall from the cliff of Brightfell tips. They let the wind wrap them up like cocoons before butterflies. And when they crash down the thick branches of the trees, the sky tears apart into an explosion of stars. Planets sprinkles like milkstains on the marble kitchen island. Suddenly, they were in an apartment without any light on except the yellow street light that flashes into the room via the window. Nails scratch on the table and the sound of jeans on skin, too suffocatingly tight against the glass top.

"I do not realise people would dream something this simple." Terror dove her fingers in the curtain of Dream's hair.

Nightmare

Dream dragged her nose against the soft skin of Terror and let her scent fill her lungs. Terror smelled like thunderstorms, like forest fires, like secrets of the ocean, like the burn inside an orphanage's throat as it cried and wailed. Intoxicating. But her question was too interesting to skip over. The answer was that it is not a dreamscape. Sometimes the line between dreamscape and reality is so blurry that they exist at the same time. Most of the time, it manifests in the back of someone's mind even when they are still awake. Sometimes to call it a dream is that simple. Dreams do not have to be krakens with tentacles as long as a bridge nor a spider crawling up the leg of a paralysed person. Sometimes dreams could be an empty apartment with no one and the only sounds are the muffled techno music one's neighbour is blasting and the breath that solidified in the air from a lover's mouth.

Like all things in the book of Time and Power, they come to an end.

The knife that was wet with Power's blood came to take Terror. They were afraid that Dream had grown too powerful and lawless. Their price was to restrict Dream into one realm only, locking her inside the dreamscape.

Dream and Terror were stuck in two different worlds. Her grief crashed like a tsunami that quaked the ocean bed. Her guttural scream shook every tree in the forest until they drained off the colours. Dream was wounded with loss that she unleashed on everyone else. She raged nightmare in every sleeper, sending them the fear of closing their eyes. She introduced every cliff, every free fall, every suffocating living grave, every drowned victim crawling on the ground but their lungs were filled with water. She made people relive the burning pyre and the delicious smell of perfectly roasted flesh and let them sweat over the sickening desire of hunger.

But when did Dream ever know its limits? Terror was her destination.

If she couldn't find the passageway between real and dreamscape, she would travel through dreams. She sought out for the people that needed dreams the most, revenge and greed.

A Girl On A Boat

Dream came to the prayer of a girl in the belly of a slaver ship.

She whispered to the Undead God. She always believed that if one said his true name, he would be more likely to answer them. People tended to pray for an easy and painless death, or for a blessing from a dead family member. But she prayed for more. In the dark cell, she prayed for the head of the Emperor. She wanted to see his blood. She prayed for the strength that would get her out of here, and back on the battlefield. And finally, she prayed for the War God.

She prayed for destruction.

Destruction came to her in the glittering image of a deity. In the belly of the ship, only the mortal girl could see the lawless Goddess as they both pursued an impossible mission.

"Let me pass through." Dream demanded. "And you shall have what you seek."

The girl allowed the deity to step into the mortal world, using her as a vessel. This was something people did not understand about Dream. She knew no limit. There was no way to chain her in one realm as she would go the distance to tear the barriers apart.

Later, the ship encountered a storm.

A giant octopus rose from the depth of the ocean to claim its victim. White wave heads roared higher than the sky. The moon orchestrated the ship to snap in half. The oars swung dangerously in the wind, slamming into the heads of terrified sailors. The octopus slapped its tentacles on screaming people and devoured them in one gulp. Those who jumped off the ship hit the water like a plank of concrete. At the tip of the boat, they saw a girl standing with her arms stretched out as rain plucked her skin. Her eyes dimmed and her body swayed on top of the rail.

But she wasn't afraid.

The only thing one should be afraid of was the power of a dream.

Dreamscape extended into the mortal realm, guiding Dream's feet as she slipped into the plane of existence that was created to solely keep her out. One must know not to contain Dream.

After all, who had ever succeed in trapping Dream?

The Squire of the Forest

Finally, Dream met the greedy.

Dream met a man in a rabbit mask. He wore a white tunic and a black yukata, unbounded at his belt. He stood looking at her from the slits of his mask as the wind picked up around them. His short black hair was messed up. The rabbit was white, with a blooming flower painted on the forehead. He wore a pair of earrings in the same lavender colour of the flower. They jingled in the wind. Take, take. They sang. Give, give.

"Squire of the Forest." Dream addressed him. "Tell me where she was taken."

The Squire of the Forest regarded her for a moment longer. Behind the mask, his expressions were shielded, but Dreams displayed no emotion either.

"Do something for me." He spoke, his voice was the rustling of the grass as the wind moved between them.

"Name your price."

Careful, careful. Said the wild flower. Price, price.

"Let the Forest take."

Dream ran in the direction the Squire had pointed her. Behind, she left a gap between dreamscape and the forest's reality. At her wake, skeletons shook and bones were picked up by invisible hands. The jaw crackled as the bones clicked together to rise. Higher, higher. The forest claimed the death as a part of its cycle. Higher, higher. The ground swallowed up to claim the rotten meat of the animals and smash the spines into fine white lines. Come, come. Its quake reshapes it into a path. Come, come. A path that would lead straight toward the new creature of death that wore the drape of fallen black leaves. Its face was the skeleton of a mountain goat with the burnt flesh of a direwolf. The man stopped in front of its body. He picked up the bloody meat and let the grime run down his fingers. He brought it to his mouth and savoured the tang that swirled in his tongue. He gave the creature life by eating it whole. The lure of the forest would forever be led by the Squire with the rabbit mask.

After all, revenge and greed were what Dream sought after. She needed their desperation to feed in her power, so she grounded herself more in the mortal realm. And when all that was done, she would be on her way.

Dream's Price

Far away in the no man's land. A dungeon was buried deep underground. It was made of bones and spirits, tied together by the vocal cords of those that lost their voices. A cage was built specifically to trap Terror, using her own devices against her. It was damped with desperation and the scratch that seared inside the lungs of a person held under water. Surface was within reach, but it could as well as being up in the sky, for it was out of reach. They were effective spells to make a cell tangible.

"You'd better run," Terror sneered. "Before the others come."

Her curtain of black hair fell around her. Her scalp was red and her fingertips were blue. Her bony shoulders rose like two towers around her head. She was a creature to be terrified of. A predator that never learnt to be hunted.

"What are the others?" A man demanded.

"I can't tell you," she spoke slowly. "I can only tell you they are a force of nature. Their eyes are as bright as my baby's."

Her voice was soft as a feather and her golden eyes glared deeply into the man's soul. He was too startled by the spark that he did not know how her lips were curving up.

"Their fire is as cruel as my baby's."

He resisted a chill but goosebumps broke on his skin. She had come so close, her hands were gripping at the bars of the cell. Her voice was smooth like velvet, slipping through the gaps.

"Their cold cuts as deep as my baby."

Her lips had turned into a wicked smile. She considered the man for a moment and remained as still as a shadow. Suddenly, her arm sprung out and she snapped at him. The bar held her back, but the man yelled and stumbled backward in surprise. His back slapped against the wall and he slid down onto the ground. Terror laughed echoing in the hall.

"Half as terrifyingly beautiful though."

A wind blew out the candlelight. Darkness engulfed the dungeon.

Dream has arrived.

Story 4
THE DAY OF SKYFALL

The Day of Skyfall

This is how the story ends. Power died, Time continued their dance alone.

"Have you ever wondered why history repeats itself?"

The first time they killed me was supposed to be the end. But you came back.

"I refused to move on, knowing what they did to you. Instead, I found a trick within myself, the trick that allowed me to live untouched by the Celestial Animals. A trick for me to be with you again. I waited for you to return, to take shape again before I found you."

"How could you do that?" I cried, "how could you live with all those memories inside you? How do you not feel tired?"

You were made of memories. I was made of broken promises.

"I do not always have memories of who we were." You said, reaching for me as I laid my bloody head in your embrace. "But this time I do. I just wanted… I just wanted you to know I will never leave you behind, I will always find you. I will always try."

"You are wonderful." I spoke softly. "Because of you, we lived a thousand times."

Because Time was not linear. Time allowed us to be everyone, everywhere, all existing in the same moment. And the next decades. And the next centuries too.

"I have loved you. I have loved you in every single life."

Time sobbed. Tears oozed from your eyes. Tears and crying were such mortal's things. Us deities did not understand fully what they were, so sorrows brought you closer to our creations.

"I'm sorry, I failed you again." You whispered.

"Don't say sorry."

You pressed your lips together, looking for something else to say. In the end, you gave up. "I'm sorry."

Epilogue

"Instead of apologizing, say you love me." I touched your face but somehow only wet it with more of my own blood. "Thank you for worrying about me and I love you."

You leaned down and touched your lips to my forehead. A thousand years of history passed between your kisses. I saw myself as a star elf, bleeding golden blood on the hand of the Titan. When your lips found mine, we were not just the black-haired boy and his bloody hands clinging onto a soul that was already leaving. We were the history of the entire humanity.

"I love you so much. I love you immensely. I love you endlessly. I love you completely. I really love you. I love you the most in the world. I completely, madly love you."

But the thing that tied it all together, I thought, was not just the mere Time or Power. It was the thing that ran between the rocks and the trees, between the particles of water, between every passing of any creature of Life. It was the thing that made someone go back in time over and over again, even if it meant watching their love die over and over again. It was stubborn desperation. It was enough faith to cling onto one good promise. Love. If there is one thing we created, it would be Love. Love and all its variations. Selfishness, selflessness, envy, desire, jealousy, empathy. Hatred. Soulmates.

If there is one thing I want to remember, I want to remember that Braia was made with you and me. Braia was made with Love.

According to many ancient texts and prints, the Day of Skyfall arrives when the Spirit evokes all of its power to humanity. On this day, the rules of nature will fall apart. Blizzard in Badar and Kyran will burn. Love becomes hatred. Brothers kills each other. The dead crawls up on the cliff of Kahasad. Dreithei surrenders to the tsunami as the ground swallows up Aler. And light will be snuffed out from Ligtia once and for all. All chains will break. All pain will be eternal. The whole world will witness Mistress Power returns from the dead with The Stranger. When she raises her arms, a blade of Fire will wipe out everything we have ever known.

V. NGHIEM

V. Nghiem is a writer with a passion for crafting immersive high fantasy worlds. Drawing from a diverse background in data science and a specialized LL.M. in finance, Nghiem brings a unique blend of analytical prowess and creative storytelling to her works. With a keen eye for intricate world-building and a meticulous attention to detail, her narratives transport readers to realms where magic and adventure intertwine.

Visit my author page on story.one:
story.one/en/author/victoria-nghiem

Loved this book?
Why not write your own at story.one?

Let's go!